Dear Reader,

I was inspired to write this book because my heart goes out to the teens out there who have ever been bullied, as well as those who have experienced low self-esteem, abuse, and/or depression. According to the National Institute of Mental Health, "In 2012, an estimated 2.2 million adolescents aged 12 to 17 in the U.S. had at least one major depressive episode in the past year."[1] Sadly, that number does not include those who smile and pretend that everything is fine, while deep down inside, they are hurting.

Maybe you are reading this and you have never experienced any of those things. That's great, BUT you never know who around you just might be! My advice to you is to be kind to others! Your kindness might be the one thing that gives them hope and encourages them to keep pushing. You don't want to be the reason why someone makes the regretful decision to end their life.

On the other hand, if you are experiencing any of those things, I want to personally let you know that you are not alone! Don't let your mind trick you into thinking that you are! So fight, don't give up, and reach out to someone for help! It is my prayer that you read this book with an open heart and that you finish with the overwhelming feeling of hope for tomorrow! Remember, your current circumstances are only temporary! So please don't deal with those circumstances in a permanent way. As long as you have hope, you have the ability to change your life! NEVER lose hope!

God Bless You All!

-Mrs. Ernestine Hopkins

*This is a work of fiction. Names, characters, places, and incidents either are a product of the author's imagination or are used fictitiously.

SAVING MYSELF FROM ME

ERNESTINE HOPKINS

ISBN-13: 9781500935351
ISBN-10: 1500935352
Library of Congress Control Number: 2014915409
CreateSpace Independent Publishing Platform
North Charleston, South Carolina

To my husband, Donald Hopkins Jr.,
my father, Ernest Kennedy,
and my mother, Opral Kennedy

———————————

A special thank you to
D. Gregg, A. Powell, K. Scott, T. Lewis, and S. Cooper
for their selfless contributions to this project.
I am eternally grateful.

CHAPTER 1

THE GREEN GIANT

"**G**et your skinny butt out of the way!" I heard a girl behind me shout as I walked to my next class. I foolishly hoped that she was talking to someone else, but deep down I knew exactly who she was speaking to. Embarrassment crept up my back as I continued to walk.

"Maybe if I just keep walking, no one will realize that she's talking to me," I thought to myself.

Before I could finish my thought, she made it clear to the entire school who she was talking to. I could feel her breath on my neck as she leaned in close to me and yelled, "What are you, skinny AND deaf?! I said get your skinny butt out of the way!" Her voice echoed through the now silent school hallway.

Fear and anger filled my heart as those words left her lips. Who was she? She was Samantha. She had been bullying me since middle school, but I was always too afraid to say anything back to her. I once saw her grab a girl by her neck and lift her off of her feet. It was as if she had super-human strength. As I watched from a distance, I decided that day that I would do whatever I needed to do to avoid her. As the memory flashed in my mind, I decided that the best course of action was to move out of her way. QUICKLY!

As I moved to the right to let her pass, I heard other kids whispering and laughing. Everyone was looking at me, but no one stood up for me. After she passed by, I locked eyes with Leila, the only person not laughing. The look in her eyes told me that she felt sorry for me, but like me, she was too afraid to say anything.

I needed an immediate escape from the embarrassment so I rushed to my next class and found a seat at the back of the room. I was relieved that I could finally exhale. I was one of the few students who actually enjoyed Ms. Neidelmier's history lectures. Each day, as she taught us something new, I would close my eyes and pretend that I was actually back in those moments of history. For the next 52 minutes, I planned to escape my horrific reality, or so I thought.

Something about this day was different. I just couldn't stop thinking about what happened before class! She had embarrassed me plenty of times before so what made this time so different? I kept rehearsing over and over what I planned to do if it happened again. It made me feel better to do this even though I knew deep down that I would never actually stand up to her.

"Ringgggggggggggg!"

I nearly fell out of my seat when the bell rang. I was so caught up in my day dream that I didn't realize that it was time for class to end. When the bell rang, I was right in the middle of punching Samantha in the middle of her mouth (since she had such a hard time keeping it shut).

In an attempt to avoid another run in with her in the hallway, I remained at my desk and pretended to arrange my binder and notebooks in my backpack.

"Is everything ok?" Ms. Neidelmier asked when she noticed that I was still there.

"Yes mam," I replied as I stood up and grabbed my bag. I figured I had stalled long enough. It was time for me to face the "Green Giant." That's what I called Samantha in my head. I called her that because she towered over me, had a short choppy haircut, and always wore green.

I peeked into the hallway and quickly looked to my left and my right. Much of the hallway had already cleared out because the warning bell had already rung. I didn't see the green giant so I rushed to gym class. I really didn't want to be late again because Coach Clark had already told me that if I was, he was going to call my mother. I didn't want that because my mother was pretty strict! I would be in a world of trouble if he called her. Thankfully, I stepped in the gym right as the bell rang.

"Well, well, well. Guess who decided to show up on time!" Coach Clark said sarcastically. "Hurry and go dress out."

"Yes sir," I replied as I rushed to the locker room. I wanted so badly to explain to him why I was almost late, but I was afraid that it would somehow get back to the green giant. What if she chose to retaliate outside of school? The teachers and principals couldn't protect me out there. Plus, what would the other kids think if I snitched? I pushed the thought to the back of my head as I scurried to change my clothes.

"At least for now I'm safe from her," I mumbled as I breathed a sigh of relief.

"Hey there *skin and bones,*" I heard a voice say.

I turned around slowly to see the green giant standing in the locker room. In that moment, I felt like my heart stopped beating and I couldn't breathe. I was in such a hurry to get dressed that I didn't even notice that the green giant had been standing in the corner the entire time!

As I struggled to catch my breath I managed to ask, "What are you doing in here?"

"The counselor's had to change my schedule, so it looks like you and I are going to get real close," she said.

She began to walk towards me, moving so quickly that it was as if she floated across the room. She stopped in front of me and stared down at me for a moment. I didn't know what to do, so I just looked back at her with chills going down my spine. Then out of nowhere, she grabbed my shoulder and punched me in my stomach! I was in complete shock because this was the first time she had actually hit me! I could tell she had been waiting for that moment. Below the evil wrinkles of her eyebrows, there was a slight grin on her face. She was enjoying this.

"You're going to feel my fists every day unless you bring me a couple of dollars.....EVERYDAY," she snarled. Then she gave me one final push as she floated out of the locker room to the gym. I wanted to crawl in a hole and die. Even though we were the only people in the room, I felt so humiliated. I tried to regain my composure before I entered the gym. As I straightened out my body, I could feel soreness from the knot in my stomach where she hit me.

When I walked into the gym, the group of girls standing with the green giant immediately started laughing. I knew that she must've told them something about me because they were all looking in my direction as they laughed.

"Ladies and gentlemen! Now that Ashley has finally decided to join us," Coach began as he looked in my direction, "we can begin our activity for the day. Today we will be relay racing. I'm going to divide you into two teams. The team that wins the most races does not have to dress out tomorrow!"

Everyone was pretty excited because we hated our stupid gym uniforms. After Coach divided us up, I was happy to find that the green giant and I were on different teams.

I really liked relay races. Running was one of the few things I was actually good at doing. When I ran, I always pretended that I was at the Olympics bringing home the gold medal for my team.

It was finally my turn to race. I could still feel the knot in my stomach. I glanced over at my opponent, but I wasn't too worried about losing because I had beaten her several times before.

"Let me go next! I want to go against *her*!" the green giant demanded as she shoved her way to the front of the line.

Lots of thoughts began to swirl through my head. "No, no, no! Why won't she just go away??? Should I let her win?? If I beat her, she's going to really let me have it tomorrow!"

"On your mark!" the Coach yelled. "Get set!" My heart began to pound. The knot in my stomach began to throb as if to plead with me to let her win.

"Go!!!!!!!" As the final word left Coach's lips, I decided that I may not have been able to beat her in a fight, but I was definitely going to beat her in that race. I was going to show the green giant what these "skinny" legs could do.

Mentally I had become Jackie Joyner-Kersee. She is ranked among the all-time greatest athletes for track and field. As I became Jackie in my mind, I no longer saw the gym or the green giant. Instead, I saw myself out there on that track with the crowd shouting, "Ashley, Ashley, Ashley! USA, USA, USA!" It felt like my feet had wings as I ran full speed ahead. I didn't even feel the knot in my stomach. All I felt was victory patting me on the back. As I crossed the finish line, I turned around to see that she had not even made it halfway to the finish line. Before I knew it, I was laughing out loud as I watched her struggle to finish. The very same girls, who were laughing at me as I walked in the gym, were standing back at the start line with their mouths hanging wide open in disbelief. Meanwhile, none of the other onlookers dared to laugh at the green giant's feeble display of athleticism. If they did, they knew they would become her new target.

When she finally crossed the finish line, she was breathing heavily and could barely stand up straight. She was bent over as if *she* had a knot in her stomach from being punched. She made her way over to me and faintly whispered, "You're going to pay for this! Instead of a couple of dollars tomorrow, you better bring me five dollars or else!"

Then she turned around and walked away. After gathering as much breath as she could, she yelled across the gym, "I let her win! I felt sorry for her pitiful butt…walking around here looking like a skeleton!" Predictably, the other girls started laughing on cue.

Even though I had to bring her five dollars of my allowance the next day, winning that race was worth it. I will never forget the day I made the green giant eat my dust!

CHAPTER 2

THERE'S NO PLACE LIKE HOME

While walking home after school that day, I looked up at the cloudy sky. I could feel cold rain drops falling on my face. As usual, I forgot to grab my umbrella, even after my mother told me that it was going to rain that day. All I could do was smile.

"What a perfect end to the perfect day," I mumbled to myself.

It didn't take long for me to become soaking wet. I ran the next few blocks home laughing at myself as I wiped the water from my eyes to see where I was going. As I approached my street, my laughter was interrupted by a familiar sinking feeling, fear. I carefully peeked around the corner to see if my step father's blue pickup truck was still in the driveway. I breathed a sigh of relief when I saw that the driveway was empty.

After I got out of my wet clothes, I went to check out my secret stash of money. I had been saving for months to get my mother a ring that we saw once at the mall. When she tried it on, her face immediately lit up. She reluctantly gave it back to the sales man because of the price. I couldn't wait to see her face when she found out that I bought her the ring! Although my mother was strict, she was still very loving and took very good care of me. She was one of the few people in my life who never left me. As I thought about my mother, memories began to rush to my mind.

As I thought back, I counted five years since my dad was home with us. He left when I was nine years old. Up until that point, he and I were really close and he was my protection. He called me his *Miracle Baby* because the doctors didn't think I was going to make it. My mother had many complications during her pregnancy. When I finally did make my grand entrance into the world, my father was filled with joy. Before my father left us, I was always smiling and laughing. I thought that we had the perfect family. But little did I know that there was no such thing as the "perfect family."

I'm not sure when it all started, but I noticed that my parents began to argue more and more frequently. I remember times when my father would stumble into the house late at night smelling of booze. My mother would ask him where he had been, but he never explained himself. He would tell her that he was a grown man and that he didn't have to answer to anyone. This would always kick start huge arguments, so things went from bad to worse. Looking back, I could see that our family was headed the right way for a dead end.

Then unusual things began happening, like we started receiving random phone calls. Our phone would ring, but when we answered, the person on the phone wouldn't say anything. They would also leave long messages of nothing but deep breathing. After becoming irritated enough, my mother stopped answering the phone and turned off our answering machine.

Many times I would be outside playing with my friends and I would notice a woman driving a yellow Chevy Corvette past our house. She drove by so often that I began to expect it. One day, to my surprise, my father pulled into the driveway driving the very same Corvette that I had seen driving by for months. He got out of the car with a big grin on his face and exclaimed, "Hey *Miracle Baby*! Do you like Daddy's new car?"

"Yes," I said reluctantly as I looked at his "new" car. I had so many questions, but I didn't dare ask.

It wasn't long after that day that my father came home and told us that he was leaving. "He was leaving us???" My heart dropped to the floor. That moment would change EVERYTHING. I was so upset with my father for not loving us enough to stay. To me, he had committed the ultimate betrayal. I felt like he loved himself more than he loved us! The man in my life, my father, my protection was leaving. To make it worse, I later found out that when he left us, he left with another woman; the woman who drove the yellow Corvette.

My entire world was turned upside down. For months I cried myself to sleep. I would close my eyes and pretend that I was Dorothy from "The Wizard of Oz." I would pretend that all I had to do was click my heels three times and say, "There's no place like home." I opened my eyes in hopes that things would be back to normal, but that never happened.

About a year later, my mom started dating Mr. Ricky. He was always super nice and tried really hard to impress me, but deep down something about him just didn't feel right. In my heart of hearts, I secretly hoped that my father would come to his senses and put our family back together. It wasn't until after he married the woman in the Corvette that I realized that my chances for that were pretty slim.

Mr. Ricky eventually proposed to my mother and they too were married shortly after. He wanted so badly for me to call him Daddy, but I refused. After all, I had a father already. Why would I need two? He became increasingly angry about the fact that I didn't call him Daddy.

"She's disrespectful!" he would tell my mother. "She is refusing to do what she's told!"

My mother would always calm him down. She would stand up for me and tell him to give me more time to get to know him. She promised him that once I came to love him like she did, I would desire to call him Daddy on my own.

Summer came and my mom found out that she would now have to work the late shift. This made me uncomfortable because I was used to my mother being home at night. So needless to say, I was not happy about it. One night after she left for work, I was in my room reading a book. I was interrupted by the sound of faint tapping on my door. Before I had a chance to respond, I heard my door click open and Mr. Ricky let himself in.

"Hey *Miracle Baby*! It's Daddy!" he said.

I sat up and stared at him with a look of confusion. I couldn't understand what he could possibly want at that late hour. After a moment of staring at one another, he turned and left my room with a defeated look on his face. I was completely disgusted. How dare he call me something that only my father called me! Why couldn't he just leave me alone? Little did I know, that night was just the beginning of his many late night visits. He continued to test the waters for a few more nights until he finally got the courage to do what he came to do.

He would start off by complimenting me and then he would make himself very comfortable in my personal space. With each encounter, he became more and more comfortable, and in turn, he became more and more inappropriate. He told me not to ever tell my mother because it would break her heart to find out what I had done.

"What I had done!?" I thought to myself. "I didn't do anything! It would break her heart to find out what you've done!" I screamed in my head. I didn't know what to do. I thought about running away almost every night, but I knew that would tear my mom a part. I carried the dark secret all alone. I didn't tell anyone what Mr. Ricky had done to me. I looked forward to leaving my house. Even if it was just a trip to the grocery store because I knew I would not have to see him for a couple of hours.

One day at school, I heard a rumor that another girl in class was being molested by one of her family members. "That is disgusting!" I heard some girls say. "Why didn't she say anything? She must've liked it!" another girl said. I knew at the very moment I heard those girls talking, that I could never tell anyone what happened to me. Everyone would think that it was MY fault. Maybe it *was* my fault. Maybe I did something that made him think that I wanted this to happen. I was so confused.

There were times I would go outside to play with my neighbors. I found myself suggesting to my friends that we play "games" like the ones that Mr. Ricky and I played late at night. Why was I doing that? I knew it was wrong, but I felt like I couldn't help myself. My emotions were so unstable. I would go from laughing to crying, then from crying to laughing. However, the emotions that I felt the most often were shame and fear.

Mr. Ricky's visits went on for weeks. When he would enter my room, I would pretend to be sleeping as not to acknowledge his presence. I would close my eyes and say under my breath, "There's no place like home," but when I opened my eyes, nothing had changed. Unlike Dorothy, my reality was that I was already at home. Ironically, I hoped that there was a place out there that was not like this "home."

One day, my mom's job asked her to work a double shift. That night he came into my room like he had been accustomed to doing. What he didn't know was

9

that this particular night, I decided that I had had enough. I lied in bed with the phone in my hand, ready to call the police if he tried anything. As he opened the door and crept in, I sat up and showed him the phone. It was pulsating in my hand because of my rapid heartbeat. I screamed in desperation, "LEAVE ME ALONE OR ELSE I'M CALLING THE POLICE!!" He put both of his hands up, backed out slowly, and closed my door. The late night visits ended.

After a few days, I would occasionally catch him staring at me. I could tell that he wanted to try again. However, as quickly as he would look is how quickly he would be reminded of that night. He was now afraid and he never attempted to come back to my room again. The same fear that was in his eyes was the same fear he placed in mine all those nights.

"Ashley! I'm home!" my mother said, bringing me back to reality. I quickly put my stash of money away. She came into my room, hugged me, and kissed me on the forehead.

"How was school?" she asked.

"Uhhhhhh, it was okay," I replied.

"Did you pray today and read your bible?" she asked.

"I was juuuuuuust about to," I fibbed.

Mother made sure that I prayed and read a chapter of my bible daily. I didn't really like to because I didn't always understand what I was reading, but I did as I was told. Every day I prayed the same prayer:

"Dear God,

There's no place like home.
Please take me back home.

Amen."

CHAPTER 3

SAVING MYSELF

"**U**ggggghhhhh," I moaned as my alarm clock went off. I absolutely hated waking up early in the morning. I often wished that we could have shown up at school whenever we felt like it. After getting dressed, I made sure to grab the five dollar bill for the green giant on my way out. I was on the lookout for her all morning. Surprisingly, I didn't even see her in the hallway like I usually would.

"Maybe she's absent today?" I thought to myself.

Another day went by, and still no sign of her. I started to think that she changed schools, but then again, I couldn't have been that lucky. By the third day, she arrived at school looking as though she hadn't slept all week. She wore her usual attire, a green shirt and khaki pants, but her shirt looked a little dirtier than usual.

She rolled her eyes at me as she passed by in the hallway as if to say that she didn't have time for me at that moment.

"Whew," I thought to myself. "That was a close one." Maybe she decided that she's going to just leave me alone since I beat her so bad in that race?

Boy was I wrong. I strolled into the locker room on time, and there she was.....waiting for me.

"You got my money?" she asked.

Without even saying anything, I handed her the five dollar bill. She flashed a fake smile at me and left the locker room. I followed shortly after.

"Hey Sam! Where have you been?" one of the boys from my class asked her. "I've been looking for you! How did it feel getting beat by Ashley the other day?" he laughed.

The green giant began to blush. The look in her eyes quickly changed from embarrassment to anger.

"Like I said the other day," she began, "I *let* her win. I mean look at her! It should be against the law for her to wear shorts in public. Her legs look like two twigs," she laughed.

Here we go again. Why did that stupid boy have to say anything to her? Sigh. I quickly walked away hoping that this would make her stop.

"Listen up everybody! Free time out on the field!" Coach yelled.

I ran outside to the little tree out on the other side of the field. Because I had ran so quickly, my pony tail came down. As I began to fix my hair, I saw the green giant and her friends walking towards me as they laughed.

"Girl...you look just like that tree you're standing next to!" she said while holding her stomach. "As a matter of fact," she chuckled, "you look like a tree that's combing its branches!! What boy would ever want you?"

The group began to laugh loudly at my expense. Once again, I caught eyes with Leila. She was the only person not laughing. In escape, I turned and ran away. Without thinking, I ran off of the campus all the way to my house.

Thankfully, I always kept my key on a chain around my neck. I unlocked the front door, ran to the bathroom, and locked myself in.

"Why does she keep doing this to me?" I wondered. "What did I ever do to her?"

I stared at myself in the mirror and examined my face and body. I let down the remainder of my hair that was only partially in place.

"She's right you know," I said to my reflection. "No boy would ever want you...I mean look at you! You're ugly, you're skinny, and you're worthless. You might as well just end your life while you're ahead. Just end it all!" I didn't realize that as I talked to my reflection, my voice became louder and louder. So loud that I startled myself!

The house phone began to ring, so I had to temporarily end my rant. I sprinted to the living room to check the phone. I saw that the number was from my school. I quickly deleted it from the caller ID *and* the message that followed. There was no way I was going to let my mother find out that I skipped the second half of school.

After deleting the message, I went to my room, lied across my bed, and cried myself to sleep. When my mother came home, I got up to pretend to read my bible like she instructed and prayed afterwards:

"Dear God,

Tomorrow has got to be better because I just can't take it anymore. If it's not better, I'm ending it all.

Amen."

The next day at school was okay. It could've been worse. The green giant met me in the locker room and collected her money. On her way out, she pushed me. The day after, on the other hand, was a different story. As I walked to Ms. Neidelmier's class, the green giant tripped me and caused me to fall and drop all of my things in front of everyone. To make matters worse, I fell flat on my face. I could feel the cold, hard tile floor pressed against the right side of my face. The impact knocked the wind out of me. Leila tried to step forward to help me, but the giant told her to back up. I looked up to see if any teachers were near, but the giants friends were busy distracting the two teachers who were close enough to actually see what had happened.

While trying to stand up, I accidentally dropped my books again. I bent over with my hands on my knees and just stared at the ground covered with my books and papers. I could hear the laughter and taunts of the crowd around me. It was in that moment that something in my head snapped.

"I'm going to get them…..ALL of them," I mumbled. "I'm even going to get the people who are just standing by watching….not helping….leaving me to fend for myself. They are all going to pay." As I spat out those words, before I knew it, I had a big wicked grin on my face. The thought of making them all pay brought me so much joy. This included the teachers who seemed to be too blind to see what was happening to me. How could they be so stupid?

"Why is she smiling?" the green giant asked her friends. "She must like falling," she said as she came over and pushed me down again. This time she kicked my books so that I couldn't reach them. I looked back at the green giant from the ground. My eyes were locked on hers. "I'm going to get her with a smile on my face," I thought. The warning bell rang so she turned and walked away. Leila walked away as well with her head down. As the hallway began to clear, one of the teachers noticed that I was on the floor, so she finally came over to help. "It's about time!" I mumbled disgustedly. I couldn't wait to get as far away from this school as possible.

That day when I got home, I only pretended to read my bible and pray. Instead, I plotted out what I planned to do to everyone at school. I needed to weigh my options. I had heard about school stabbings, shootings, and bombings, but I wasn't sure which one I actually had the courage to try to pull off. Plus, the thought of getting caught frightened me.

I heard about other school massacres where the police were able to trace everything back to a certain person. How could I do it without getting caught? Maybe I could wear a mask and a body suit or something? I needed to get to the public library and do some research.

I told my mom that I needed to do some research for a school project. I knew it was the perfect lie for her to be willing to drop me off, and it worked. I stayed at the library until it closed. I researched everything from buying a gun to unsolved crimes. By the time I left, I still didn't know exactly what I was going to do, but I was okay with that. It made me happy to know that I was one step closer to getting my revenge….to giving everyone exactly what they deserved.

On the car ride home, my mom asked me if I was doing okay. She noticed that I was different, but she couldn't quite put her finger on exactly what it was. "What happened to your face? It is swollen baby, does it hurt?" she asked.

"I'm fine mom," I told her.

"Well, I noticed your face AND you seemed a little distracted while you were reading your bible earlier. Let's read it together when we get home," she said. I sighed in my mind. She ruined my plans. I wanted to have my plan of attack together by the end of the weekend. "I'll just have to work on it after I finish with her," I thought.

When we got home, my mother and I sat at the table and she handed me an ice pack for my face. "Let's read Proverbs Chapter 20," she said.

For most of the chapter, I was daydreaming about my big plan until my mother read something that caught my attention.

"Wait….can you read that again?" I asked.

"Sure….verse 22…..Do not say, I will repay evil; wait for the LORD, and He will save you."

As my mother continued to read the rest of the chapter, I was sitting in shock by that verse. It was one of the few times that I clearly understood what it meant. It kind of felt like that verse was speaking directly to me, but I wasn't sure.

Afterwards, I went directly to bed. While lying there I kept replaying the day's events over and over in my head. So many thoughts were going on at once that I couldn't focus on one detail. I decided to try and pray for real this time:

"Dear God,

Even though I understood what that scripture meant, I'm completely confused. How do I know that You will save me? I've been fighting alone for so long and You haven't saved me yet. How long do I have to wait? I don't know if I can wait any longer. If You won't save me, I think I'm going to try to save myself.

Amen."

CHAPTER 4

A LOT ON MY MIND

"**W**ake up sweetheart," I heard my mom whisper in my ear as she lightly patted me on my back.

"Why is she waking me up? Isn't it Saturday?" I murmured in my mind.

"Get up and get dressed honey, we're volunteering downtown today," she continued. After a quick breakfast and my morning hygiene ritual, we were on the road.

We pulled in front of a building with a big sign on the outside. It read, "Battered Women's Shelter."

"What are we going to do?" I asked nervously.

"Whatever they ask us to do," she replied, as she grabbed my hand and escorted me to the building.

When we arrived inside, I was shocked by the huge amount of mothers and children. It was so sad to see so many of them displaced. My mother began to talk to a few different women. I was always amazed at how easily they would open up and share their stories with her. It was like they trusted her instantly.

While she talked, I slipped away and began to wander around the building. While walking, I heard a faint whimper in the distance. I followed the sound until I found where it was coming from. There was a young girl who looked to be about ten years old hiding underneath a table crying and clutching an old blanket. I got on all fours and crawled under the table with her.

"Hi, my name is Ashley…what's yours?" I asked.

I waited patiently for her to answer, but she remained silent. I could see that she was afraid.

"Are you here with someone?" I continued. She still did not answer. I continued to talk because I figured that would make her open up. I told her about my favorite color, my favorite things to do, and how much I liked her blanket. Before long, the tears slowed down and she was actually smiling.

"Where's your mom?" I asked.

"She's gone," she replied. Her smile quickly faded.

"Where did she go?" I asked.

"I don't know," she replied, while putting her head down.

"Is she coming back?" I asked.

After a few moments of silence she spoke again.

"When we lived in our house," she began, "my mom would leave and wouldn't come back until the next day. I would still get up and go to school so that I could eat because there was no food at home. When mom came back, she acted weird. She didn't act like mom. She would just sit on the couch and stare at the wall. The other day, the rent lady came knocking on our door. She told us that we had to go, so we came here. Mom left me again, but this time, I don't think she's coming back. She gave me a long hug and told me to hide under the table. She told me not to move until after she was gone, so I just stayed here……..but I'm so hungry," she finished, as she grabbed her stomach.

"Stay here," I told her as I got up to go find my mom. She quickly grabbed my arm and said, "Please don't leave me." I took her by the hand and we both went to find my mom.

We found her sitting on a cot and talking to a woman wearing a blue shirt. I patiently waited for them to finish talking.

"My husband and I have been married for 15 years," the woman said. Something about this woman looked familiar, but I couldn't figure out what it was. "But what nobody knew," she continued, "is that he's been hitting me for the past 10 years….I'm surprised that I'm even still alive! There were times that I thought he was going to kill me!"

"I'm so sorry to hear that! Do you and your husband have any children to-gether?" my mother asked.

"Yes, a daughter," she replied while wiping tears from her eyes. "For years I've tried my best to keep this secret from her. I didn't want her to know that her father was a monster. Plus, I never knew either one of my parents. I always dreamt of getting married, having children, and living happily ever after. I didn't want to take that dream away from my daughter." She began to cry intensely. My mother lovingly embraced her.

After she pulled herself back together, she continued. "Lately it has gotten worse. He used to only hit me after my daughter went to bed. Now he hits me in front of her. He told me he was going to kill me and that my daughter needed to see her mother plead and beg for her life!"

"In front of your daughter?" my mother shockingly asked.

"Yes," she paused and looked down at her hands. She began to twiddle her fingers nervously. "When he told me he was going to kill me, he swung back his arm to strike me, but my daughter ran and jumped on his back. She was yelling 'Leave her alone!' He was so angry that he slammed her into the wall, but that didn't stop her from trying to save me. While he was punching me, she jumped in front of him to block me from his blows. That's when he...he hit her. I saw my little girl's body collapse at the power of his punch. My heart broke into a thousand pieces. That's when I knew that enough was enough. The next morning when he left for work, I grabbed my daughter and got out of there! I didn't even take any clothes or anything! I swore to her that I would never let him hurt us again."

"You are a brave woman, and you did the right thing by coming here," my mother exclaimed. "Where is your daughter now? Is she here?"

"She is," she replied. "But I don't want him to know where we are since he threatened to kill me. I kept my daughter out of school for a few days because I figured that he would try to find us there. I didn't know what else to do so I let her go back to school. I didn't want her to get behind."

Hearing her story tore me apart. I thought I had it bad because I had a bully at school. At least I had a warm bed to sleep in.

"Where is my shirt?!?!" I heard a young girl shout in the distance. The woman wearing the blue shirt immediately jumped up and ran to the girl's aid.

As she was returning back to us, I heard her say, "I know baby, but it's for the best. That shirt was dirty and had holes in it. You look great in this new shirt that they gave you. You look just fine."

I turned around to see who she was talking to and what I saw blew my mind. The young girl that she was comforting, her daughter, was the green giant!

We locked eyes and before I knew it, I said, "Green...I mean Samantha???"

She was not wearing her usual green shirt. Instead, she wore a pink shirt with flowers all over it. She looked at me with tears in her eyes and ran away.

"Excuse us," the woman in the blue shirt said as she ran after her daughter. I had never seen the green giant cry before. I didn't even know she was capable of crying. I turned to see my mother looking at me as if to figure out what was on my mind. However, the young girl's hand I was still holding caught her eye.

"And who is this beautiful girl you have with you?" mother asked me.

"Mom, we have to help her," I began. I told the girl to sit down while we talked. I explained to my mom everything that the girl had told me. My mom's expression changed from a smile to a look of concern. She immediately walked over to the girl and gave her a long, tight hug. The girl melted in her arms.

"I'm going to get you some help," my mother told her.

She grabbed her hand as they walked to find someone who worked there.

I sat on the cot and waited for her to return. I was still amazed at how many women were there. I wondered how many other women and children had common stories as to why they were there. After over an hour later, my mother returned. When she saw the concerned look in my eyes, she put her arm around me, smiled and said, "Don't worry, everything is going to be fine....let's go."

The car ride home was pretty silent. I had so much on my mind. I felt so bad for that sweet girl. How could her mother leave her like that? Where did she go?

"Mom what's going to happen to her?" I asked.

"Well, I'm not for sure. Most likely she will be sent to an orphanage. They will probably try to find her foster parents and eventually get her adopted," she replied.

"Can we adopt her?" I asked with excitement in my voice.

"Oh, I don't know about that sweetheart. I'm not sure how Ricky would feel about that," she replied.

"Mr. Ricky," I sighed.

I wish I had the courage to tell her what he had done. I didn't think about Mr. Ricky more than a few seconds. My mind was overwhelmed by all I had seen that day, starting with the green giant. For the first time, I actually felt sorry for her. I had no idea that she and her family were going through so much. I wondered if maybe since she knew that I knew her secret, she would be nice to me. Maybe I wouldn't have to go through with my plan? I decided to bring her money to school on Monday just in case but I did really hope that she was going to treat me better than she had been.

When we got home, my mom reminded me to read my bible and pray:

"Dear God,

Please protect that sweet girl from the shelter, and help her to get adopted by a loving family.........and (I hesitated) please help Samantha's family.

Amen."

CHAPTER 5

WAITING

For the next couple of days, every time I woke up, the green giant was on my mind. The look on her face when she saw me at the shelter was heart breaking. Her look told me she had no intentions of her secret getting out. I couldn't believe that I actually prayed for her!

I remembered hearing that it said somewhere in the bible that you should love your enemy, but that was a tough one because I definitely didn't love her! As I got dressed for school, I began to think about what I planned to do when I saw her at school. Before I left, I made my final decision. If she didn't bother me, then I would not go through with my plan.

⋏

As I walked down the hallway, I was prepared for the worst. I kept expecting her to jump out of a corner and lunge at me at any moment, but she didn't. I cautiously looked over my shoulder. I was doing whatever I could to avoid a surprise attack. Then I saw her, standing at the end of the hall, wearing a new blue shirt. She was talking to her friends, but the entire time she was watching me with her arms folded. After the warning bell rang, she ended her conversation and walked into her class. She continued to watch me the entire time.

I walked the rest of the way to my Math class, but I refused to let my guard down. I had prepared myself for a surprise attack from her, but it didn't happen. As I sat through class, I tried to figure out what my recent encounter with the green giant meant. Did it mean that it was over? Maybe she was trying to figure out the same thing? Time would tell.

The day went on and it was finally time for P.E. class….the moment of truth. I peeked into the locker room, but I did not see her. I walked in and changed my clothes….still no sign of her. Maybe she's no longer the green giant? Maybe she's just plain old Samantha now?

"You tell, you die," I heard a female voice say.

"Who's there?" I asked while trying to figure out where the voice was coming from.

I saw no one.

"You know who I am, and you know what I'm talking about," she said. "Leave my money on the bench and go," she finished.

I did as I was instructed.

As we did our activities in the gym, I occasionally glanced over at her, trying to figure out what she was up to. She actually seemed to be her normal self. I could barely focus on the activities because I was so focused on her. Before I knew it, class was over. As we were leaving the gym, she came from behind me and shoved me violently into the wall. Before I had the chance to stand back up straight, she came behind me and said, "Just in case you thought I was playing about our little conversation earlier," and walked away. As usual, her friends laughed. I stood there motionless. I absolutely hated being publicly humiliated.

"You see God! Did you see what happened to me? They deserve what's coming to them!" I said. Then all of a sudden, the phrase "love your enemies" popped into my head. As a matter of fact, those three words kept replaying in my mind for the rest of the day. When I got home from school, I decided to do a little research online to figure out where exactly in the Bible it says to "love your enemies." I was pretty excited when I found it. Luke 6:27-28:

*"But to you who are listening I say: Love your enemies,
Do good to those who hate you, bless those who curse you,
Pray for those who mistreat you."*

"But I don't understand. Why should I 'bless' people who treat me bad?" I asked aloud. I continued on to read verse 35:

*"But love your enemies, do good to them,
and lend to them without expecting to get anything back,
then your reward will be great,
and you will be children of the Most High,
because He is kind to the ungrateful and wicked.
Be merciful, just as your Father is merciful."*

I understood what the scripture meant, but I just couldn't figure out how I was supposed to be kind to her when she kept treating me the way that she did. I sat on my bed, struggling with the difficult decision of whether or not to continue working on my plan.

That night, before bed, I prayed:

"Dear God,

If this is what You really want me to do,
then please show me a sign. I know that I shouldn't ask for a sign, but it would be really be
nice if You gave me one.

Amen."

⋏

The next morning I was awakened by the sound of my alarm clock whaling. I wanted to pick it up and throw it out the window. I did not want to wake up at all. I felt like it was just another day for me to deal with the same stuff. On one hand, I wanted to try to do the "right" thing, but on the other hand, I also wanted to do something really crazy to make them all pay. I had so much anger inside of me and I was tired of life all together. I was tired of waking up each night to make sure that Mr. Ricky was not trying to pay me a visit. I was tired of only seeing my father every other weekend, I was tired of not having any friends, I was tired of feeling ugly, I was tired of feeling worthless, and I was tired of feeling trapped. I was just plain old tired.

I thought that maybe I should just pretend to be sick and stay home. My motivation was on level zero. I just wanted to lie in the bed all day. I just needed some time to not have to worry about the green giant, school, and everything else in my life.

Convincing my mom that I was too sick to go to school was not hard to do. She even stayed home for a bit to make sure that I had everything I needed.

"There's soup in the fridge if you get hungry. Call me if you need anything," she said as she walked out the door. As soon as the coast was clear, I climbed out of bed and went to the bathroom. I thought maybe I could use this time to create a new look for myself. However, while I stood in front of the mirror all I could do was to critique myself. I saw everything that they said was wrong with me and I could do nothing to change it. In my mind I could just hear the green giant saying, "What boy would ever want you?"

The truth of the matter was, I actually agreed with her. I believed no boy would ever want me. It seemed like all the other girls at school had a boyfriend. They were always holding hands and looked so happy. I believed that if I had a boyfriend, I would've been happy too. The problem was that none of the boys wanted me. I could tell because they didn't even look at me. On top of that, my mother wouldn't even allow me to have a boyfriend.

As I stared at the mirror my mind began to wander. I remembered how I used to have this huge crush on this boy named Greg. I would see him around the school, but we had only spoken to each other once during a class we shared. One day, my teacher sent me to return a book to another teacher's class. As I walked down the hallway, I began to fix my hair and clothes because I knew that Greg was in that class. Excited about the opportunity to see him, I decided that I would take a chance and flirt with him. When I arrived at the classroom door, I paused outside for a moment to correct my hair one last time for my grand entrance.

I opened the door slowly and poked my head inside. To my surprise and delight, I immediately saw Greg. I was so excited to see him, and it meant the world to me to know that he saw me too. When our eyes connected, it felt like time stood still. I was anxious to hear what he would say to me. "Are you looking for someone?" he said. Without hesitation, I looked at him with a smile on my face and said, "Yeah....you." I winked afterwards like I had seen a lady do in a movie once. I expected him to smile back or come out to talk to me. Instead, he scrunched up his face in total disgust and said, "Huhhhhh?!?!" My face was on the floor! I definitely was not expecting that response!

To try and save the embarrassing moment, I laughed and replied, "Just joking!" I entered the room, gave the teacher the book, and quickly exited the room. Once outside the room, I slammed my back against the lockers and put my hand over my face. I was so embarrassed. That was an epic fail!

After that experience, I came to the conclusion that I would probably be single for the rest of my life. The green giant wasn't telling me anything I didn't already know.

"No boy would ever want me," I said as I turned the bathroom light off, went back to my room, and slept the day away.

That night I told my mother that I felt better and that I was well enough to eat dinner with her and Mr. Ricky. I was actually tired of being in the bed all day. We all sat at the table eating and listening to mom go on and on about her day. Blah, blah, blah, boring, boring, boring. My mind began to wander.

All of a sudden, I felt a foot rub up against my foot. I moved my foot over and continued eating. Seconds later, I felt the foot again. This time the foot started sliding up and down my leg. I looked up at my mother, but I knew it wasn't her because she continued talking. I looked over at Mr. Ricky and he continued to look down at his plate, pretending to cut the same piece of steak over and over again. I was disgusted. "May I be excused? I feel nauseous," I said.

"Sure sweetheart, I'll be in to check on you in a few," my mother replied.

As I got up from the table, I stepped down hard on his big toe.

"Ouch," he moaned. I walked away with a huge grin on my face. On my way to my room, I heard him making up some story to my mother about why he moaned. Every time I thought about what Mr. Ricky did to me I felt so ashamed and disgusted with myself. How will I ever get past this?

That night before bed, my prayer was short:

"Dear God,

(Sigh) ....

Amen."

CHAPTER 6

LOOKING FOR A SIGN

The next day at school I was determined to see a sign that I should actually "love my enemy." Even though I understood what the scriptures meant, I was not convinced that loving my enemy was the way to go. Especially considering the way I was being treated. The green giant was definitely the enemy that I needed help to love.

Every time I began to think that maybe I should give loving my enemy a chance, the giant came and changed my mind. A perfect example of this was during lunch time that day. As I entered the cafeteria, I was reminded of how lonely lunch time was since I usually ate by myself every day. I would find a table that was far away from the giant and her friends. While I ate quietly, I imagined that the table was filled with my bestest friends. We joked and laughed about our day and made plans to go to the mall after school. I figured that this day would be no different. I stood in the long lunch line and jealously looked at the other kids who seemed to be having the time of their lives.

"Hey Ashley," I heard a voice say behind me.

"Hi," I replied as I turned to see who was speaking to me. I was surprised to see that it was Emily. Emily was a very pretty and popular cheerleader. She was the girl that all the guys wanted. She basically was everything that I wasn't. I couldn't believe she was actually speaking to me!

"I noticed that you're always sitting by yourself. Do you want to sit with me and my friends today?" she asked. I looked over at the table where she normally sat. All of her friends, including the green giant were waving and smiling at me.

"Sure!" I replied. I couldn't stop smiling. I didn't know for sure why they were being nice to me, but I thought that maybe that was the sign that I was waiting for. I felt that things had finally turned around.

"Look at that girl in front of you," Emily whispered in my ear as we waited in line. "Don't you think she looks disgusting?" I didn't agree with her, but I didn't want her to treat me differently if I told her what I really thought.

"Yes," I whispered back. I was immediately overwhelmed with guilt. I had said the exact same thing about someone else that the giant had been saying about me. Emily started laughing and said, "You should pretend to bump into her and make her drop her tray on herself." I suddenly got a lump in my throat. I didn't want to do that!

"That would be so embarrassing for her but so funny for us! Do it!" she continued.

I wanted so badly to fit in that I would've done anything. I decided to go along with her plan. As the girl walked towards her table holding her tray, I bumped into her. She tried to catch her balance, but in doing so, she ended up dropping the entire tray on herself and another girl. The cafeteria quickly filled with laughter. I felt so bad about what I had done. I immediately bent over and helped her pick up her food.

"I'm so sorry," I kept whispering to her as I helped.

"No you're not! I heard you with Emily in line. Get away from me!" she replied.

I got up and walked towards Emily's table to join my new friends. "Get away from our table you idiot!" the green giant said. I looked to Emily to understand why the green giant said that to me. I was pretty confused, but she cleared it all up for me when she smiled and waved goodbye. As I walked away I heard the green giant say, "Thanks for doing me a favor by making her drop her tray." I felt like such an idiot and I quickly walked away. Some of the kids at the other tables saw the entire scene and laughed and whispered as I walked past them. I couldn't believe that I did something so stupid. I was so embarrassed that I dumped my tray and left the cafeteria without eating my food. I went to the bathroom and closed myself in one of the stalls until my lunch period was over. I sobbed the entire time. I promised myself that I would never trust anyone at school ever again.

After the lunch period was over I cleaned myself up and went to Science class. Mrs. Garcia told me that we were working in groups of three for our Science projects. The day before, while I was absent, she allowed the students to choose their own partners. I was glad that I wasn't there for that because usually, no one wanted me to be in their group. Mrs. Garcia told me that I was in the group with Leila and Greg. I immediately got butterflies in my stomach. I thought that I no longer had a crush on Greg, but I guess I still did!

When I sat down to join them, Greg didn't even look up at me. He continued to write in his notebook and didn't seem to notice that I was even there. Leila smiled and said, "Hi Ashley."

"Hi," I replied while looking down at the Science project instructions.

"So far, we've only chosen the topic. Yesterday we made plans to go to the library after school today. Do you think you can come?" Leila asked.

"Sure, I just have to call my dad and let him know to pick me up from the library. It's his turn to have me this weekend," I replied.

"Your parents are divorced? My parents are divorced too," Leila said.

"So are mine," Greg chimed in. I tried not to look shocked when he spoke up. I didn't think he was paying attention to us. I did notice that he seemed to be a little uneasy. I thought maybe he was still freaked out by me winking at him.

The conversation continued and I found myself looking forward to going to the library after school. We agreed to meet at the flagpole when the last bell rang to walk over to the library. I secretly couldn't wait!

⋏

After school, Leila and Greg were waiting for me at the flag pole. We walked quietly at first until Leila broke the silence. "So why are your parents divorced?" Leila asked as we walked.

"My father abandoned us," I responded bitterly. "And you?" I asked.

"My parents had me when they were sixteen and got married when they were eighteen. My mom says that it didn't last because they were not ready to be parents or married. What about you Greg?" she asked.

"Well....my parents divorced because my mom always used to hit my dad. She was angry because she felt that my father cared more about his career than our family. My father was a real man, so he never hit her back. One day, he just got tired of her mess, so he packed up his stuff and left," Greg replied.

I had no idea that his mother hit his father. I didn't know what to do or say. All I managed to say was, "I'm so sorry."

"It's cool," he replied. "I just want to make my Pops proud, you know? Graduate and become successful." I was surprised to find out what Leila and Greg were going through. They always seemed to have it all together. Up until that point I had always felt like I was the only person going through real problems. To me, everyone else looked so happy and perfect in their lives. For the first time in a long time, I didn't feel alone. When we arrived at the library, we found a table and sat down.

"Before we start, there's something I need to say," Leila began. "When I first found out that you were going to be in our group, I was pretty upset."

I couldn't believe that she said that to me. I had always thought that she was a nice girl, but maybe I was wrong.

"Not because I didn't like you," she continued, "but because I was ashamed of myself," Leila finished.

"Why?" I asked, with a confused look on my face.

"Because....I have just stood by and watched Samantha torture you. I haven't even told a teacher or anything. I was afraid of what she might do to me if I did....and for that I'm sorry," she replied. I could tell that my getting bullied was something that really bothered her because she had tears in her eyes.

"Well, I saw her messing with you, but I never thought to jump in and help," Greg said. "I mean, I was like, you weren't fighting back, and Samantha is a chick, so why should I...you know?" he said.

"I guess I can see your point of view. I never really thought about it like that. I just thought that nobody cared," I replied.

"Why do you let her do that to you? I know you will get in trouble for fighting, but you could at least tell someone!" he said.

"Because....I'm afraid of her!" I replied. "I saw her choke a girl once. Imagine what she'd do to me!" I exclaimed.

"Well, you've got to stand up for yourself or tell your mom or dad or somebody! There's no way I would let someone do that to me. I wish my Dad would've stood up for himself sooner," Greg said with sadness in his eyes. It was obvious that he was still sad about his father leaving.

We sat talking for so long that before I knew it, it was time for my dad to pick me up. Where did the time go? This was the most fun I'd had with classmates from my school since I was in elementary school. We agreed to meet again after school on Monday.

"She's actually pretty cool," I heard Greg whisper as I walked away. His words lifted me off the ground. I was smiling from ear to ear.

When I walked outside, my smile faded. I was pretty shocked to see my Dad's wife, Linda, outside waiting for me. She was driving the infamous yellow Corvette. I rolled my eyes and took a deep breath. I wanted my dad to pick me up, not her. I did not like it when he did stuff like that. It was as if he tried to force me to be close to her. I was always nice and respectful when I saw her, but there were so many questions and concerns I had about her. For instance, why did she choose to be with *my* father? I once saw a talk show where a woman said that she didn't know that her boyfriend was actually already married. Was that the case for Linda? Why did she choose to stay with him once she found out he was married? I wanted to ask these questions, but I figured that she would get pretty upset, so I didn't. During the car ride I sat mostly silent as she talked about any and everything. I responded with the occasional, "oh really?" and "okay." It took everything in me not to jump out of the moving vehicle and roll on the asphalt like the police officers do in movies. By the time we arrived to my Dad's house, I was extra anxious to see him.

"Happy early birthday!" she exclaimed as we walked through the door. Inside there were lots of gifts, decorations, and a cake. I was pretty surprised because my birthday was a few weeks away. My father entered the room with his arms stretched out to hug me. I ran to him and embraced him tightly. He whispered in my ear, "Linda did all of this for you. I didn't have anything to do with it. This was all her."

He always went out of his way to tell me what she did for me. I believed it when he said it, but I felt like she tried to buy my love and forgiveness with gifts. She really was a nice lady, and if it wasn't for that situation, I probably wouldn't have had a problem with her.

That night we all went out to eat my favorite type of food, Mexican. To me there was nothing better than authentic Mexican food. We went to a small place that I'd never been to before. The food was really good. While we ate, a woman walked over to the table and said to my father, "Bryan? I haven't seen you in years! How have you been?"

My father hugged her and said, "I've been fine, how about yourself?"

"I've been well. Where's your beautiful wife tonight?" she asked as she looked around the restaurant as if she was looking for my mother.

Uh oh….this was awkward. I looked over at Linda's face to see how she took all of that. She had a smile on her face, but I could tell that she was very uncomfortable. As my father explained to the woman that Linda was his "new" wife, Linda proudly stood up and shook the woman's hand. My father was her most prized possession. I wanted to be happy for them, but I just wasn't ready to yet.

I thought back to before my parents were divorced. We lived in a beautiful house. After the split, my mother couldn't afford to pay for the house on her own. She kept it for as long as she could, but it eventually became too much for her to handle. I was so sad when we moved because we moved away from all the great memories of the house and all of my best friends.

I never will forget the night that my friends and I had a sleep over and we prank called my father's house. We took turns calling and hanging up when she answered. "Hey, I've got an idea," one of my friends began. "This time when she answers, Ashley should say '*Home wrecker!*' before she hangs up the phone." After much convincing, I agreed.

Ring Ring.

My heart was pounding as the phone rang. I felt that maybe I shouldn't do it.

"Hello?" I heard a woman say. "Hello???" she said a second time. My friends were motioning for me to say it. It was now or never.

"HOME WRECKER!" I yelled as I hung up the phone. We all laughed so hard that our stomachs were hurting. It felt so good that we decided to do it again!

Ring Ring.

"Hello!" My father yelled as he answered. "I don't know who this is calling my house but you better not call here again!" He said as he slammed down the phone. We quickly hung up the phone and were rolling around on the floor as we laughed. I never told my father that it was me, although deep down inside, I was sure he already knew. My thoughts returned to my present moment. I watched my father introduce his new wife to the lady; I couldn't help but giggle under my breath as I thought about the time that I called her a home wrecker.

That night as I lied in bed at my father's house and reminisced on how my day went, I smiled. I realized, for the first time in a long time what it felt like to not feel lonely. I still was not sure how to love my enemy, but could Leila and Greg's friendship with me be my sign that everything was going to be okay? I thought about that until I fell asleep. I was actually hopeful about the future.

CHAPTER 7

COURAGE

The weekend flew by, and before I knew it, it was Monday morning again. I didn't want to admit it, but I actually had a good time with my father and his wife. On my way out the door, I double checked my pocket to make sure I had the green giant's five dollars. When I arrived at school, I immediately looked around for her. As usual, she was in the hallway talking to her friends. This time, she was wearing an orange shirt. I assumed the shelter must've given her some new clothes again.

"Why are you wearing all of these different colors now?" I heard her friend ask as I walked towards them.

"Yeah...why are you?" I asked as I took the five dollars and placed it in her hand in front of her friends.

"Why is she giving you money?" another girl asked.

"Good question," I replied as I walked away. Talking to Leila and Greg had given me a little confidence. I could tell by the look on the giant's face that I was going to pay for that later, but I didn't care. I walked away with my head held high and a grin on my face.

Later, when I walked into the locker room, I was mentally prepared for something to happen. I knew that there was no way that she was going to let me get away with our previous encounter. Sure enough, after the locker room cleared out, the giant came running in and slapped me right in my face! "Don't you *ever* do that again!" she growled. "Tomorrow, you owe me $10!"

I quickly regained my composure and asked, "Samantha, are you doing this because your family needs money?" I must've been too loud because she quickly grabbed me by my shirt and pulled me into one of the stalls. "That's none of your business and you better bring me my money tomorrow!" she whispered. Then she shoved me, causing me to fall on the toilet and walked out.

After she left, I rushed to the mirror to examine my face because it was still stinging where she hit me. My cheek was bright red and for the rest of the day, all I kept hearing from everybody was, "What happened to your face?" I was upset with myself for letting this happen to me again and I knew that it was finally time for a change. As I walked home after school I thought, "The giant wants to play that game? Fine! Two can play that game!"

The next day, I marched right up to her, and threw the $10 at her. She caught the money before it fell to the floor and before her friends noticed. She lowered her eyes at me in anger as I walked away. On one hand, I wanted to find a way to "love my enemy." On the other hand, I wanted to stand up for myself and humiliate her the way she humiliated me, regardless of the consequences.

For the rest of the day, I found ways to avoid encounters with her. For example, I managed to skip gym class by telling Ms. Neidelmier that I needed to go to see the nurse. By the time school was over, I was exhausted from all of my "ducking and dodging." Usually when school was over, I would walk out of the front entrance. This day, I decided to switch things up by using one of the side exits. Once outside, I peeked around the corner before going to the flagpole to meet Greg and Leila. We were meeting so that we could walk over to the library again. The coast seemed to be clear so I quickly jogged over to the flagpole.

"Hey sticks!" I heard from across the street. I turned around to see the green giant and her friends laughing.

"Hey skyscraper!" I yelled back as we walked away. I immediately felt bad for saying that to her. Being mean just wasn't me. I had been feeling so much pressure from Greg to stand up for myself, but I was pretending to be something that I wasn't. I wished there was a way for me to stand up for myself without tearing her down.

"It's about time!" Greg said as we walked. "I can't believe you actually stood up to her!" I wondered what he would have said if he knew that she has been hitting me and she was the reason for that red hand print on my face yesterday. He probably wouldn't have encouraged me to stand up to her in that way, I thought.

⅄

That Friday night, I stayed the night at Leila's house. We had so much fun. Her mom ordered pizza and we stayed up all night talking and laughing.

"Leila….can I tell you something?" I asked hesitantly.

"What's up?" she asked.

Tears began to stream down my face. I stood up and walked over to the window. I could feel her gaze locked on me as she anticipated what I was going to say. "I hate myself and I hate my life," I said.

"Why???" she asked.

"For a lot of reasons! I hate that my father's gone, I hate my step father, and I hate the way I look," I rattled off.

"What!" she exclaimed as she stood up. "Girl, have you looked at yourself lately? You're gorgeous!"

"No Leila, no I'm not! 'Sticks' and 'skin and bones' are all I've ever heard! I'm so sick of being laughed at, so sick of being picked on, so sick of Samantha and her friends, so sick of it all. I hate my life!" I replied as I looked out the window.

"Girl, she's just jealous. That's what jealous people do. They try to tear other people down….that's what my mom always says. Plus, if you were ugly, Greg wouldn't have such a big crush on you," said Leila.

"What?!" I said, as my tears immediately stopped.

"I said Greg has a crush on you. You're a pretty girl. Being thin doesn't mean you're ugly. My grandmother always told me that the thing that makes a girl unattractive is not her face but her lack of self-confidence," she finished.

"Now come on!" she said while grabbing my hand and pulling me to the middle of the room. "Let's practice our confidence walk!"

"But I don't know how to walk with confidence!" I replied as I pulled away and walked back to the window. Leila grabbed my hand again and pulled me back to the middle of the room. She practically forced me to put on her mother's high heels. I never knew that Leila could be so aggressive! We walked back and forth across the room like we were runway super models. The funny thing was the more we did it, the more confident I felt. During one of my super model strides, I tripped and fell to the floor. But instead of being embarrassed, I couldn't stop laughing. When we finally settled down, I asked Leila, "Do you ever miss your father?"

"Yeah….I do a lot," she replied.

"Does it ever make you angry that he left?" I asked.

"It used to," she replied. "It hurt deep…..once I got past my anger, I was finally able to see how much happier my parents were without each other. My grandmother helped me to see that my father didn't leave *me*….he left the situation. He was unhappy, but I guess he deserved to be happy too."

Her words hit me like a ton of bricks. I never wanted to admit it before, but my father *was* much happier in his new life. I thought back to the night that my father, his wife, and I were at the Mexican restaurant. I remembered how proud he was when he introduced her as his new wife. I then realized that I needed to forgive them and just let them be happy.

"So why do you hate your step father?" Leila asked, interrupting my thought. I immediately stopped breathing. Why did I bring him up? I had not told anyone about him and I was not ready to talk about what happened yet. Plus, what if she had the same reaction that the girls at the school had? What if she thought the whole thing was *my* fault?

"Ummmm…..I'll tell you about him another time," I said as I turned to wipe away a new onset of tears. I guess Leila could hear that something was wrong in my voice. She sat up and said, "What's wrong Ashley? What did he do? Did he ground you or take away your phone or something?"

I couldn't speak.

"Do you want me to get my mom?" she asked. I shook my head 'No.' I could see the look of desperation in her eyes as she pleaded with me to tell her what was going on. My heart began to beat rapidly. I was so afraid of what I was about to say. It was my secret, but I realized I could not carry it any longer.

"It is worse than being grounded. I haven't told anybody this but.........he used to come into my room at night and do things to me," I said.

Leila began to cry. She wrapped her arms around me and we cried together. I was amazed at how it seemed like she actually felt my pain with me.

"Ashley you have to tell your mom," she said as she reached for her phone.

"No! I can't tell her something like that over the phone," I replied.

"Okay, but you have to tell her! He's a dangerous man! Even your mom is not safe with him!" she exclaimed. "You have to tell her when you go home tomorrow! Do you want me to go with you?" she asked.

"Yeah, but you have to promise to act normal until *I* get ready to tell her.... okay?" I demanded.

"Okay," she replied. I knew at that moment that if I didn't tell my mom, then she would. I tossed and turned almost the entire night. I was so nervous about finally having the courage to tell my mother. I closed my eyes and counted sheep in my head until I finally fell asleep.

ᛉ

I arrived home the next evening shortly before dinner time. Mom said it was okay for Leila to come over for dinner. At first, I was going to talk to my mother privately, but we decided to tell her with him present so that he couldn't deny it. We waited until we were all at the dinner table.

"Soooooo," my mother began, "how was your sleepover?"

"It was good," I replied. Mother was so happy that I had a friend now. She had a big smile on her face. I felt bad that I was going to make her lose that smile in the next few moments. Then all of a sudden, I felt a foot going up and down my leg. I immediately knew who it was. I kicked his foot off of mine, but he didn't catch the hint. He did it again. I looked over to Leila to see if she noticed. She looked at me and motioned for me to tell my mom what was going on.

As his foot slid up my leg again, I stood up and blurted out, "Mom! Mr. Ricky came into my room at night and did things to me!" she dropped her fork and looked up at me. "What?" she said in a low voice.

"He told me not to say anything," I replied.

"Virginia! You don't believe this do you? She's lying...she's just making this up because she doesn't like me. Baby, you know the girl doesn't like me!" Mr. Ricky pleaded with my mother.

"Now Ashley....you don't have to make this up just because you don't like him. Sweetie these are some serious allegations," said my mother. I couldn't believe my ears! Did she really just suggest that I was lying? Did she really believe him over me? Leila walked over to me and squeezed my hand.

"Mom...he would come into my room every night when you worked the late shift. He only stopped because I threatened to call the police," I said. She covered her mouth. By this time I was practically yelling every word. "Just a second ago, he was rubbing his foot up and down my leg. I kicked his foot off but he wouldn't stop!" I cried.

"Get out!" my mother screamed. For a moment, I thought she was talking to me because Mr. Ricky remained seated. My mother got up, grabbed the phone, and made a call. I didn't know who she had called until she said, "Yes.... my name is Virginia Peterson and I would like to report the abuse of a minor." She believed me! Thank God!

"I'm not going anywhere!" Mr. Ricky shouted. "This is my house and I know what I didn't do! I'm not going to run like I'm guilty! I'm innocent! She's a liar!" He pointed at me as if to say, "I'm going to get you for this." He looked and sounded so convincing. If I didn't know the truth already, I would've believed him!

"Ashley, take your friend to your room until I call you back out," my mother said sternly. I was afraid to leave her alone with him....what if he hit her or something? From my room we could hear them arguing, and I began to question whether or not I made the right decision by telling my mom.

Once the police arrived, Mr. Ricky really began to throw out a bunch of lies. By the end of the night, he left the house wearing hand cuffs. Shortly after, Leila's mother came and picked her up so that my mother and I could be alone.

"Bye and thank you for everything," I said to Leila before I closed the door. I walked over to the couch and joined my mother. We sat silently for a few minutes. I could hear the faint sound of my mother weeping. "I am your mother," she said quietly. "It's my job to protect you. I can't do that if you keep secrets sweetheart. You should've told me," she said as she wrapped her arms around me. I cried in her arms. I finally felt safe. As she rocked me back and forth, I prayed to God:

"Dear God,

*Thank you for giving me the
courage to tell my mother.
Please heal her broken heart.*

Amen."

CHAPTER 8

DECISIONS

T he next morning, I woke up in my mother's arms. I still felt so bad because I knew how much she was hurt by Mr. Ricky. He brain washed me for so long. He actually convinced me that my mother would be upset with *me* if she found out what *I* had done. I cannot believe that I actually believed him! I looked at my mother's face as she slept. Her eyes were swollen and puffy from being up so late and crying. Her hair cupped the shape of her face. Even in her pain, she was still beautiful. She was such a loving and kind person. She didn't deserve that. When her alarm clock went off, I thought she would silence it and return to sleep. I figured that she would want to stay home, considering everything that happened the night before. Instead, she turned off the alarm and said in a sleepy voice, "Let's get ready for church."

I stared at her for a moment as I tried to read her. I wanted to figure out if she was angry with me. If she was, she was pretty good at hiding it because I didn't feel anger from her at all. Strangely, she seemed at peace.

"How are you so calm?" I asked her.

"Because….I am confident that God is going to take care of me. God's going to take care of us! I know this because he did it before so he'll do it again," she replied. Wow….her strength was amazing. I sat on the end of the bed and stared out the window and watched a hummingbird as it tapped on the glass. I thought about how bound by fear and regret I had been for years. I decided that from that day forward, I was going to make sure that I always felt as free as that hummingbird. I thought about how scared I was to tell my mother for so long. In an attempt to walk away from fear, I decided to explain to her why I chose to keep my secret from her.

"Mom, I was so scared to tell you. I didn't want you to be hurt, especially after everything you went through with Dad," I began to explain to her.

"I understand sweetheart," she interrupted. "When everything happened with your father, I completely lost it. I felt helpless and alone. My mind went to a dark place. You didn't know this, but I began to suffer from depression. I was no good to myself or to you. When I hit rock bottom, I realized that I couldn't get through that situation by myself. I had to put all of my faith in God and trust that he would guide me through. Here....I want you to read something."

She removed a plaque from her dresser. I had seen the plaque countless times; I had even read it a few times, but I never really thought about what it actually meant. It read:

> *"You will keep him in perfect peace*
> *whose mind is stayed on you,*
> *Because he trusts in you*
> *Isaiah 26:3"*

After I finished reading, she sat next to me, turned my face towards hers, and looked me in my eyes. The look in her eyes answered any questions I had concerning her being angry with me. There was not any anger in her eyes. I only saw her love for me shining through.

"You see, because I trust that God's got my back, I don't have to walk around worried and in fear of what might happen in the future. I have peace in my mind and my heart. No worries. I may be upset from time to time, but at the end of the day nothing can take away my peace," she said. She gave me a quick tight hug and then ushered me out the door to get dressed for church.

As I got dressed, I began to reflect on what her words meant to me. I wanted to have perfect peace too. I didn't want to worry or feel bad about what happened with Mr. Ricky anymore. "Here goes nothing! I trust you Lord," I said under my breath as we walked out the door.

After church, we decided to make it a "Girl's Day" out. My mother wanted to help keep my mind off of the "incident." We went out to eat and got our nails done. Afterwards, we window shopped in my favorite mall for a couple of hours. Every so often I caught my mother staring blankly as if she were in deep thought. I knew that she was still very hurt over what her husband did, but she was more concerned about my well-being. She showed so much selfless love. I told myself that when I became a mother, I wanted to be just like her.

It was late in the evening by the time we returned home. When I stepped out the car, I stopped and stared at the moon before we went inside. The air was crisp and the sky was clear. As we walked to the door, we noticed that our front door was broken off the hinges. We rushed back to the car and called the police. We didn't go in because we did not know if the person was still in-side. Within minutes, the police arrived and did a complete search of the house. Thankfully, no one was in the house, but the person did leave us a message. Two phrases were spray painted across the walls. They read, "HE'S INNOCENT" and "YOU WILL PAY FOR THIS." The entire house was ransacked and much of our property was destroyed.

"Is there anywhere you folks can go and stay tonight?" the police officer asked my mother.

"Yes there is," she replied.

The police waited while we packed an overnight bag and left. We went to stay at my older cousin's house. She lived in a three bedroom townhouse and she was a single mother with four children. When we pulled up to the townhouse, I began to think about how I used to spend a lot of time there with my cousins when my parents first separated. I had nothing but good memories there, so I didn't mind that we went there that night. As I began to take my seat belt off, my mother placed her hand on my arm and gently said, "Give me just a moment before we go in sweetheart. It's been such a long day. I need just a moment to exhale." I watched her as she closed her eyes and took in a deep breath of air. I knew my mother needed to think about something positive. As I waited, great memories of my time spent at my cousin's place began to flood my mind and I chuckled to myself.

"Mom, remember after Daddy left how you brought me over here because you had to go to work?" I asked.

"Yes.....why?" she asked.

"Do you remember the time you had just straightened my hair and told me not to play by the creek while you were gone?" I continued.

"Yes dear....I remember," she replied.

"Well.....since I'm coming out and telling you the truth about things, I thought that I should tell you something. While you were gone, my cousins and I decided to play 'who can jump the farthest' over the creek. When it was my turn to jump, I fell and the dirty water got all in my hair!" I laughed.

"What?!" my mother exclaimed. "But when I came to pick you up, your hair was still straightened!"

"That's the thing mom....cousin Joann dried my hair and straightened it with the dirty water in it. We didn't want you to know that I didn't listen," I laughed.

"Oh no!" my mother gasped. After a brief silence she began to laugh. It was so good to see her smile. As we laughed in the car, I knew that everything was going to be okay. It was going to be pretty crowded in my cousin's house, but I didn't mind. I felt so much safer there than I did at my own house. My mother and I held hands, stared up at the moon, and listened to the crickets chirp. It was so peaceful outside.

Before I knew it, I fell asleep in the car. I must've been pretty exhausted from the day's events. While sleeping, I had a dream that I was standing in the middle of the street. It was late at night and police car lights were flashing all around me. I could hear the cops yelling at me. I did not know what I had done wrong for them to be after me. I stood motionless in the street with my hands in the air. Then my mother ran up to me, stood beside me, and grabbed my hand tightly. Then slowly, the darkness of the night turned into the light of day. The cops and flashing lights went away.

Suddenly, I awakened from my dream, confused as to where I was. I had forgotten that we were right outside of my cousin's house. I wasn't sure how long

I had been asleep, but it was long enough for my mother to fall asleep as well. I woke her up and we went inside. After a few quick greetings, I went directly to my "usual" sleeping spot and I tried to go back to sleep, but instead I lied there wide awake.

After giving up on sleeping, I climbed out of bed and started to walk down stairs. I overheard my mother and cousin talking.

"Well I don't care what you say," my cousin said. "I think that message came straight from him!"

"But how?" my mother asked. "He's in jail.…I checked!"

"All he had to do was make a call to someone from jail," she replied.

Just as I was sitting down on one of the stairs, I began to feel a sneeze coming on. I tried to slowly get up and go back up the stairs but…..

"A-CHOO!" I couldn't hold it in any longer.

"Ashley?" my cousin asked.

"Yeah it's just me," I replied while walking back down the stairs. "I couldn't sleep."

"You know it's not polite to eaves drop," my mother replied while putting her arm around me as I sat down on the couch.

"Sorry….do you really think *he* had someone to do with this?" I asked my cousin.

"We're not for sure sweetheart, but don't worry everything will be fine. As long as we have each other," my mother said while smiling at me. Maybe that's what my dream meant. Everything was going to be alright, and that my mother was going to be my side. I was not completely sure, but it did sound like a great happy ending. I went back up to bed and lied down until I finally fell back to sleep.

The next morning, my mother wanted to go back to our house to get more clothes for us. She decided that it would be safer for us to stay at my cousin's place for a week or so until the dust settled. She dropped me off at school on her way to our house. I couldn't wait to tell Leila everything that happened. I actually, at that point, considered her to be my best friend. She had been there for me a lot and I felt like I was a better person because of her positive influence on me. I came to understand what the school counselor meant about a true friend making you better. "If your friend was always trying to get you to do the opposite of what's right, then they were never a true friend to begin with," I recalled her saying.

The morning flew by and it was time for gym class. My mind was so preoccupied that I completely forgot all about the green giant and her money. When I walked into the locker room, I was surprised to find her standing there waiting for me.

"Well, if it isn't Miss Smart Mouth," she said.

"Look Samantha, I know you want money, but I don't have it today," I impatiently replied.

"What? What do you mean you don't have it?" she hissed. She was so angry that I could almost see fumes coming from her ears.

"I had a really rough weekend and I haven't been home," I pleaded. "The money is at my house."

She looked down at the ground as she contemplated her next move. "Then you're going to take me to your house after school and get me my money!" she demanded.

"I can't go to my house right now, it's not safe!" I replied. I was so nervous that my hands were sweating. I thought I had the courage to stand up to her, but in that moment, while alone with her, my courage flew out the window.

"Well then, I guess you'll just have to pay me another way!" she said as she punched me in the stomach. Surprisingly, her punch didn't have the same intensity as it had before. When she swung to hit me again, I dodged it and used all my strength to push her back away from me. I pushed her hard enough for her to lose her balance and fall over the bench behind her. I ran out of the locker room as fast as my legs would carry me. I didn't understand why she still punched me when I explained to her why I didn't have the money. I concluded that I probably made her mad when I stood up to her the other day. "She still doesn't have the right to keep hitting me," I thought to myself. I had to find a way to put an end to this. I couldn't keep giving her money and I couldn't keep letting her hit me! "Maybe I should finally tell an adult like Greg suggested?" I wondered.

As I was sitting on the gym floor thinking this over, I looked up and saw the giant running out of the locker room towards me. Her arms looked like windmills as she flew across the gym. She got in my face and said, "Look...I don't care what's going on at your house. Bring me my money tomorrow, or else I'm going to beat you down in front of everybody!"

"Break it up ladies! Don't make me come over there!" Coach yelled from across the gym. The giant backed off and said, "Tomorrow!" as she walked away. It looked like I had a decision to make. I was going to bring money or be prepared to fight her the next day. As much as I didn't want to do this, I decided that I was going to fight back!

CHAPTER 9

THE ONLY WITNESS

I went to sleep with confidence in my decision to fight back, but by the time it was morning, I had changed my mind. Who was I kidding? What could possibly come out of me fighting the giant besides another episode of me being publicly embarrassed? After all, my chances of winning were pretty slim! All that would end up happening was the giant would win the fight, and would end up having the upper hand once again.

As I closed my eyes on the way to school, I pictured her tossing me up and down the hallway in front of everyone. After the fight, I would still end up giving her the money that I could've just given her in the first place. I came to the conclusion that the best thing to do was to just give her the money to spare myself the humiliation. Just as I was feeling more and more confident in my new decision, I suddenly realized that once again, I did not have any money for the green giant! "Mom, can we please stop by our house real quick before you take me to my school?" I asked.

"We really don't have time sweetheart. We're already running late," she replied. A sinking feeling came over me, and before I knew it, I was trembling with fear. To try and calm myself down, I looked out the window and began to imagine that we weren't on our way to my school. Instead, I pretended that we were on our way to the beach. I could feel the warm sun kissing my skin. As I closed my eyes, I could hear the waves as they gently rolled across the ocean.

My moment of peace was interrupted by the overwhelming fear of seeing the green giant again soon. My stomach and face both bore her signature at one time or another and I was not interested in letting her mark another part of me. I knew that telling an adult about how she treated me was the right thing to do, but I was afraid of what the other kids would think if I snitched. I thought they would respect me more if I fought her, but I wasn't sure that God would want me to do that. I struggled with deciding whose respect was more important; theirs or God's. The thought of fighting her in front of everyone made me cringe. My mind began to race as I frantically tried to come up with an alternate plan. Usually, I didn't ask my mother for things twice, especially when she'd already told me no, but that day was different. If I didn't get that money, the giant was going to kill me!

"Mom please! I forgot something really important that I need for one of my classes," I lied. Well...technically, it wasn't a complete lie. After all, I *did* need the money at school.

"No, you should've told me earlier. I'll be late for work if we stop and I can't have that," she replied in a "that's final" tone. I shrunk down in my seat as my imagination ran wild again about how the fight would play out. I was sure that once I got in the locker room and she found out that I didn't have her money, she would get really angry.

I pictured her dragging me out of the locker room and into the gym. But to her surprise, I would stand up and have the courage to hit her back. I would hit her with a one-two punch and watch her fall to the floor. Then the referee would step in and say, "Ladies and Gentlemen! We have our new Heavy-weight Champion of the World....Miss Ashley Peterson!" He would then grab my hand and lift my arm high in the air. I would smile as the crowd went wild and repeatedly yelled my name.

"Ashley! Ashley! What are you doing?" my mom said as she interrupted my day dream. "Get out of the car! I'm going to be late!" I didn't even realize that we had arrived at my school. When I got out of the car, I stood and waved goodbye to my mother as she drove away. I felt like it was *Dooms Day* and that I would never see her again. Usually, there were a lot of kids outside, but I was so late that most of the kids had already gone inside. When I walked across the grass towards the building, I heard muffled screaming in the distance. As I looked to my left, I saw a girl wrestling to get away from an older man. I looked around to see if there was anybody else around to help, but I didn't see anyone. I pulled my phone out in an attempt to record what happened.

"I said now! Get back in the car NOW!" he said as he pulled her towards his car. "No daddy! Leave me alone!" she yelled back. He pushed her into the back seat and then ran around to the driver's seat and jumped in. My hand was shaking as I tried to record the car. Thankfully, I was able to capture the license plate! When the car pulled away, I could clearly see the girl in the backseat. The girl was the green giant! She pounded her fists on the window and screamed, "Help!" As her father sped away, he swung his arm at her from the front seat, trying to get her to stop yelling.

I immediately ran towards the school to get help, but then I stopped in my tracks. I turned back around and watched the car drive away in the distance. I began to battle in my mind with what I should do. Why should I help her after all she did to me? This could've been my ticket to freedom. No more green giant meant no more public humiliations, no more fights, and no more giving up my money.

She's my enemy. I shouldn't help my enemy! Right? Then all of a sudden, out of nowhere, "Love your enemy" and "Do good to those who hate you" popped in my head again. "Ugggggghhhhhh," I moaned as I closed my eyes. Tears began to fall because I knew in my heart what I had to do. I ran inside the building and went straight to the office. After I showed them the video, they called the police, and the search for her began.

That night, pictures of her were all over the news. I was so scared and I felt so guilty that I even considered not helping her. I wondered if she saw me standing there watching as her father sped away? After I viewed her kidnapping story on the news, I confessed to my mother everything that had been happening between her and me and how I almost didn't call for help.

"I'm so proud of you for making the right decision. I know that must've been hard!" she said.

"Oh it *was* hard mom! I just kept thinking about how it would've felt to not have her around anymore," I said with extreme guilt.

"I can understand that too, but you could've avoided that by simply telling an adult so that we could've helped. You have to learn to stop trying to take on the world by yourself Ashley. You're not alone," she replied.

"From now on, I will!" I said. I still felt so bad for waiting to get help for her. When my mother saw the sad look on my face, she sat down next to me on the couch and said, "Don't be so hard on yourself. You're human and we all make mistakes. The only thing that matters is that in the end, you did the right thing. Did you learn from your mistake sweetheart?"

"Yes mam....I did," I replied. She always seemed to know the right thing to say.

"Well....we'll pray that God brings her back home," she said. We turned the T.V. off and immediately prayed for her and her family. This time I REALLY meant it. Everything that she did to me over the past few years no longer mattered. All that mattered to me was her safety.

⋏

A few days went by and they were still looking for her. The news station contacted my mother because they wanted to interview me about what I saw that day. I was really nervous about it, but they thought it would intimidate her father to actually see an eye witness speaking about the encounter on the news. I was willing to do anything to help her and to redeem myself. The news anchor and a bunch of other reporters were all over our front lawn in hopes to catch a glimpse of the girl who provided the evidence.

My mother invited the news anchor inside and after he gave me a few instructions, we got started.

"Tell us what you saw that day?" he asked.

"I saw Samantha Fuller screaming as she was being pulled into a car at the front of the school," I replied.

"What did you do when you saw this?" he asked.

"I pulled out my phone to record everything and took it inside to the office," I replied.

"That was a very brave and smart thing for you to do. How well do you know Samantha?" he asked.

"I know her pretty well. I've known her since middle school," I replied.

"Tell us more about her as a person and if they're watching right now, what would you want her to know?"

I paused for a moment as I thought about everything that happened between Samantha and me. This could've been my opportunity to tell the world about the things that she'd done. A week ago, I would've jumped at the chance to make her look bad, but after everything I'd been through, I knew better than to do that. I was not the same person.

"Samantha has been through a lot," I began. "But she is a strong girl and a fighter. Samantha if you're watching this, I want you to know that we are praying for your safe return."

"Thank you Ashely. We'll continue to keep the community updated on this story. This is Brett Thompson with Channel 5 news."

I was relieved that the interview was over and I was proud of myself for "doing good to those who hated me." That night before I went to bed I prayed for the giant:

"Dear God,

Please protect the giant until the police find her.
Thank you for giving me the strength to do the right thing.

Amen."

⅄

After they aired my interview, the word quickly spread around school that I was the one who turned in the video of the car and the license plate. I began to notice that people actually smiled at me instead of ignoring me when I walked down the hallway.

I was sitting in History class when the phone in the room rang. I watched Ms. Neidelmier as she looked up at me while she talked. After she hung up the phone she said, "Ashley, you're needed in the principal's office." Why did they need me in the office? Did Coach finally report me for being late? Or maybe he reported my confrontation with the giant several days before? By the time I arrived at the office, I still hadn't figured anything out. I was instructed to have a seat and I was told that she would be with me in just a moment.

I nervously waited and fidgeted in my chair as I thought of the worst case scenario. That was my first time being in the principal's office. As I sat there, I thought about what it would have been like to be called in her office during my senior year to discuss being the class valedictorian. However, I was certain that that was not the reason I was there. In the middle of my thought, the principal entered. She also had two other people with her; the green giant and her mother! I gasped and put my hand over my mouth when I saw them. The green giant was beat up pretty bad. Both of her eyes and her top lip were swollen. She had bruises on her neck and arms. Her mother ran over to me, hugged me, and exclaimed, "Thank you, thank you, thank you!" She looked as though she hadn't slept in days. She let me go and stepped aside so that the giant could approach me. We stood in front of each other for a moment and stared at each another. She awkwardly stepped forward, leaned towards me, and lightly hugged me. I could tell that she was in pain. Even though she was pretty beat up, I was so relieved to see her alive. I again thought that if I would've said something sooner, then it wouldn't have taken the police so long to find her. However, at that point, all that mattered was that she was there.

"Because of you giving the information about the car to the school, the police were able to track down the car. If it weren't for you, we may not have found her! Thank you!" her mother exclaimed.

"You're welcome!" I replied. It felt so good to do something good for someone else.

"Mom, Mrs. Sanchez, can I talk to Ashley alone for a few minutes?" the giant asked.

"Sure," they said. The giant's mother kissed her and looked at her lovingly for a brief moment before leaving the room. The principal squeezed my shoulder and smiled at me as she walked out. At first, we were both silent. I wasn't exactly sure what to expect because we hadn't interacted much, with the exception of her punches and my pain. Maybe she was about to demand the money that I never paid her?

The giant hung her head low and with tears in her eyes, looked at me and asked, "Why would you help me? After all that I've done to you?"

"Because," I began, "it was the right thing to do. You would've done it for me too right?" I said with a smile on my face as tears filled my eyes.

"I'm just…..I'm just so sorry," she stammered. "I didn't deserve your help. I promise after I get a job, I'm going to pay you back every penny!" she said.

"Why did you even want my money?" I asked.

"Because, we've been completely broke ever since my mother left my father. No money for food or gas," she said as she fiddled with her hair. "My mom borrowed money from my family, but she didn't want to keep bothering everybody. I wanted to help."

"But why couldn't you just ask for help instead of hitting me?" I asked.

"All I know is hitting. My mother thinks that I just found out about my father hitting her, but I've known for years. When my father wanted something done, and he meant business, he used his fists. But that's no excuse….I know that I shouldn't have done that to you…..I'm sorry," she said regretfully.

In that moment, I remembered that I *did* have some money on me! I reached in my backpack and handed her a $20 bill that was stashed in a secret pocket. Even though I needed that money for my mother's gift, I wanted her family to have it because they needed it more than we did.

"Why are you giving this to me after everything I've done to you?" she asked with a shocked look on her face.

"Because….I forgive you…everybody makes mistakes and deserves a second chance," I replied. She stared at me for a moment with amazement in her eyes and then she hugged me tightly. As we hugged, I noticed that she was only about an inch or so taller than me. I began to see that she wasn't really much of a "giant" after all. I realized that her "Green Giant" persona was all in my head.

Her mother and the principal joined us again and we talked for a little while before they had to leave. As I walked back to class, I was grinning from ear to ear. I was so happy that they found her.

When my mom picked me up after school, I couldn't wait to tell her all that happened. I could see the joy on her face as I detailed the exchange between Samantha, her mom, and I. I could tell that she was proud of me. To make her happy made me happy. To top off the evening, my mom gave me a twenty dollar bill before I went to bed that night. Wow! Little did she know, I was going to spend that entire twenty dollars on her, after all, she deserved it and it was the right thing to do!

CHAPTER 10

CONFESSIONS

The next weekend came and it was once again my father's turn to spend time with me. I thought a lot about my last visit with him and how my step-mother tried so hard to impress me. Some people would've taken advantage of her kindness, but I never did. I was more annoyed by it than anything else. I felt like it was finally time for the three of us to have a talk. I was nervous about doing it because I was not sure how they would react. However, Leila convinced me that I would feel much better after I talked to them. I promised myself that I would do it before it was time for me to go back home.

I stood in the hallway and listened as they talked. They laughed as they re-counted a T.V. show they had watched earlier in the day. I searched for the cour-age to walk in and say what needed to be said, but I couldn't find it. After a few minutes of going back and forth in my head, I convinced myself that it would be better to not say anything. As I turned around to walk back to my bedroom, I heard my step-mother say, "Hey Ash.....come and join us!"

I walked to the table, sat down, and began fiddling with the place mat. I was trying to build up the courage to just open up my mouth and speak. "Just do it already!" I screamed at myself in my head.

"Dad and Linda....can we talk?" I finally interrupted.

"Sure," my father said as they turned their attention towards me. I invited them to the table and we all sat down. Their eyes, filled with curiosity, were focused on me. I felt butterflies in my stomach. Even though my nervousness made it hard for me to speak, I knew I had to overcome it.

"Well….you may not like some of what I'm going to say at first, but I need to make some confessions so that I can feel better," I began. My step-mother sat up straight with a concerned look on her face. My father placed his hand on my hand as if to show me that I had his support. I began to wonder if he would still support me when I finished. I decided that it would be easier if I didn't look at them, so I looked out the window as I continued.

"You guys may not know this, but I've walked around for the past several years with a lot of anger towards you both. Dad….I felt like you abandoned me and that you were being selfish when you left," I said. He started to interrupt, but I gently asked him to let me finish. He sighed, placed his hand on his forehead and allowed me to continue.

"And Linda," I continued, "I felt like you were selfish as well because all you seemed to care about was having my father. It didn't even matter to you that a home was being broken. It didn't matter that I felt like I was losing my father," I said. I paused to wipe the tears that began to flow from my eyes and I looked at them to see if I could read their expressions. I could see anger in my step-mother's face as she bit her lip to keep herself from reacting to my words. I figured it was best to continue before I lost my audience.

"Dad, even though you have always been there for me, it just wasn't the same after you left. I felt like my confidence and my self-worth left with you that day." I continued. Their body language changed as they became more uncomfortable with my words. As my father let go of my hand, I continued talking because it was important for me to truly explain to them exactly how I felt. I had been carrying it around for years and I didn't want to carry it anymore.

"A lot has happened to me over the past few years that you guys don't know about. I know I'm only fourteen, but I feel like everything that has happened to me has shaped me into a better person. I don't see the two of you as the bad people anymore. Daddy, I forgive you for leaving. I now understand that you didn't leave me because you were being selfish. Instead, you left because you felt unhappy. And you felt that you deserved to be happy. I see you two together and I know that you are happy. That's all I want for you," I said. He looked at me with a surprised look on his face as if he didn't expect me to say that. He reached out for my hand and squeezed it lightly.

"And....Linda....I forgive you for cheating with my father. We all do things that aren't necessarily right sometimes. If I hurt someone, I would want them to forgive me and not hold it over my head. So....I forgive you," I said.

Before the last word could leave my lips, she stood up and walked away from the table. My father followed her to try and calm her down. He put his arm around her but she yanked away and said, "No! I have been nothing but kind to that spoiled brat and you're just going to stand there while she talks to me like I'm trash?" Then she turned to me and said, "Don't you ever speak to me like that again....do you hear me?" She stormed out of the room and slammed her bedroom door behind her.

My father looked at me with tears in his eyes and hugged me. "Just give her some time to think about it all. I'm sure she'll come around," he said as we hugged. I could feel his heart beating in his chest. "I know that it must've been hard for you to say those things, and even though I don't agree with *how* you said everything, I am glad that we had this conversation," he said. We sat at the table and talked for hours. I never realized that my father actually felt guilty for leaving. I really hoped that telling him what was on my heart would help him to forgive himself.

I heard their bedroom door open in the distance. I braced myself for the worst because I didn't know what to expect. Linda slowly walked back into the room where we were sitting. I could hear her house shoes slapping the floor with every step. She stood by the table where we sat, and lit a cigarette. I didn't even know she smoked. She inhaled several puffs before speaking. "After today, I'm done smoking," she awkwardly began. "As hard as it is for me to admit this, I can understand why you felt the way you did," she said.

"I apologize if what I said hurt you. I was just afraid that if I didn't get that off my chest, I would carry it around with me forever," I explained.

"Well....I *do* appreciate you for forgiving me. I never told your daddy but I did feel a little guilty. I could always tell by the look in your eyes that you were hurting and I knew it was because of me. I admit that the way your daddy and

I got together could've been handled better but I just didn't want you to see me as the enemy. I wanted you to see that I really was a good person," she finished.

"I do believe that you're a good person and I promise not to hold the past over your head anymore. Let's move forward….deal?" I asked.

"Deal," she said and we hugged. It wasn't the hug that I'd imagined, but it was a start to a better relationship.

⋏

Although we never found out who broke in, my mother and I moved back in our house. We had complete and total faith that we would be safe. Mr. Ricky was waiting to stand trial. He no longer denied what he did. He actually seemed sincerely apologetic. As hard as it was, I had to forgive him too because I allowed that situation to have power over me for far too long. If I refused to forgive him, then I was still letting that situation control me. I had always felt ashamed and worthless because I allowed it to happen. My mother helped me to see that it wasn't my fault and I was worth more than I could ever imagine. The problem I had was I tried to deal with that situation and every other situation all by myself. I thought I could handle it all on my own. I wouldn't admit that I needed help so I wouldn't seek any help. I was constantly getting in my own way.

The next week, Samantha finally returned to school. She was no longer the green giant to me. She was Samantha. She was a normal girl, like me, who had problems that she had to overcome. As I walked down the hall to Ms. Neidelmier's class, Samantha walked towards me with a smile on her face and handed me a note. "Don't read it yet," she whispered as she walked away. When I got to class, I opened it. It read:

"Dear Ashley,

When you forgave me, you taught me how to forgive!
I've been hurting for so long, but what you did for me changed my life. Thank you for keeping my secret about the shelter

and thank you for not saying bad things about me on the news.
You could've gotten even with me by telling everyone, but you didn't. I really
appreciate that!

Your friend,
Samantha

(P.S. If anyone messes with you, I'll get them for you! ☺)"

As I smiled and folded the letter back up, I thought about my journey in learning to love my enemy. Who would've thought that loving your enemy could turn into all of that? I should've done it sooner. For the longest time I went back and forth with God. I prayed for answers but the answers were right in front of me the entire time. I was just too stubborn to see them and I was too busy trying to solve things my way. I saw Samantha as a giant, but in reality the real giant that I needed to overcome was my mind.

λ

After school, I met up with Leila and Greg. We were heading to our favorite place to hang out….the library. As we walked, I glanced over at Greg. He was still so cute to me. I told my mom about how I had a crush on him. When I asked her if he could be my boyfriend, she looked at me like I had lost my mind and said, "Absolutely not!" So for the moment, we had to settle for just being friends. Friends? I couldn't believe that after feeling alone for so long, God had blessed me with friends!

While in the library, we talked about my journey as a person. We decided that we were going to the school counselors to ask if we could start a club to help reach out to kids who had been bullied or who felt alone. I really felt good about giving back and I knew that we could help a lot of kids. I didn't want anyone to feel the way that I once did.

My mother said that my experiences made me wise beyond my years. If I could have a conversation with my old self, I would have a lot to say to her. I would look into her eyes and say,

"You are perfect the way you are, so always be yourself. Live in the moment, because every moment is precious. Open your eyes and look at the world right in front of you. You are right *where* you are supposed to be and *when* you're supposed to be. You are surrounded by family. Sure…it's not the traditional family that you once longed for, but that's okay because they love you deeply. Never question your self-worth or allow anyone else to define who you are. Do not allow your thoughts to take control of your life. You are the person that God said that you are, so put on your heels and walk in confidence!"

⋏

That night before bed, I prayed to God:

"Dear God,

Thank you for the opportunity to help others who have been through what I've been through. I was the only thing standing in the way of me having a happier life. Me and my giant thoughts. Thank you for showing me how to forgive and love. Basically, thank you for saving me.......from myself!

Amen."

 **ERNESTINE HOPKINS** is a motivational speaker and an author who has a heart for helping others overcome the adversities that life has thrown their way. This desire motivated her to start Hope Speaks Life in 2014. Hope Speaks Life is an organization that empowers teens and young adults to not let their negative thoughts, past experiences, and current circumstances stunt their growth as individuals. They will learn how to let hope speak in their lives and build the courage to fight for their success in every facet of their life. She believes that one of the ways they can do this is by never giving up!

Ernestine was inspired to write *Saving Myself From Me* while teaching Middle School English. She related to several of her students because when she was their age, she too struggled with low self-esteem. *Saving Myself From Me* is one of the first of many books that she plans to write to help people fight mentally for their success! She wants her readers to be able to picture that they are the main character. As they read, it is her hope that they will learn from the characters experiences and walk away better because of it.

For more information about Ernestine Hopkins,
Hope Speaks Life, or booking opportunities, visit www.hopespeakslife.org

✦

............Eighteen. Eighteen was the number of times that we've had to move. After today, that number had changed to nineteen. I'm not sure why I was still keeping count because thinking about it only made me sad. I began to cry as I thought about everything that had happened that day, but I quieted down when I heard footsteps in the distance. I held my breath, clutched my blanket, and tensed my body as I heard the footsteps coming closer...........

✦

For release dates of
future projects by Ernestine Hopkins visit:
www.hopespeakslife.org

Notes

DEAR READER

[1.] "Major Depression Among Adolescents." *NIMH RSS*. Web. 30 Oct. 2014.

Made in the USA
San Bernardino, CA
24 February 2018